JACK THE KILLER

PRANJAL SHUKLA

Preface

I would like to thank Mradu Shukla for helping me with this book. She's my younger sister who made all the photos for this book.

I would thank Anuj Shukla for helping me with this book. He's my father to whom I use to tell all the stories before going to write and at the time he use to give me ideas and which helps me in write story.

I would thank Ritu Sharma Ma'am who is my English speaking skills, tutor. She helps me in this book indirectly as in the tuition every weak we have to make a story on our own and we have to her and this thing gives me the motivation to write this Book.

I would thank Anshu Shukla for helping me with this book. She's is my mother who gives my motivnation to write this story.

Thanks a lot to help me to write this book

Contents

Prologue

Paul - Who Finds the dead body of Kamolika

    James - The Cop Officer

    Sir Willam Hawk - The Father of Light Hawk

    Light Hawk - The Hero who catch the Slayer

    Jack - The Slayer

    Cop 1 - Who was a cop but was in the team of Jack

    Cop 2 - Who was also in the Jacks team

    Cop 5 - Who was also in the Jacks team

    Cop 6 - Who was also in the Jacks team

    Jack 2 - Who was the Burning Man

    Obheek - Who work in Jack's company but help Hawk

    Aarush - A detective who help's Hawk in finding Jack's lab

    Robert - Jack's Right Hand

CHAPTER ONE

THE BEGINNING OF THE STORY

That was a murky day and there were 4 brothers named Pranjal, Rohan, Arnav and Sam; Their winters break have arrived and on the first day they got a letter from their grandfather in which there was written that " Sons from a long time I didn't see you and what to meet you and this is the correct time you are having your winters break, so I want that you all come to my house and will enjoy a lot"

So they discuss this thing with their mom and dad

Oh, said their mom, that's a nice idea to spend time with grandfather, you all should go to his home.

Wow after a long time we will see our grandfather said Arnav in an obligated way.

Yea, so what should we do now asked Rohan

You first pack your bags and tomorrow we will send you to grandfather's house said, Dad.

At night...

All 4 brothers were too contented that the entire night they were not able to sleep.

The Next Day....

They all sat in the car and go to grandfather's house after 4 hours

They reached grandfather's home it was an old giant bungalow

Ding Dong

The gate opened and there was standing the grandfather of 4 brothers

They all hugged their grandfather.

After that, they break up at home.

Then their grandfather served them their favourite food.

They all tasted and said

Wow, baba! What delicious food you have made. Said Arnav

Arnav, grandfather always made delicious food. Said, Rohan

Grandfather laughed.

At night Pranjal, Rohan and Arnav were watching a horror movie but Sam was having dreaded watching horror films, so he go to his grandfather's room.

When he saw Sam he asked " What happen, Sam, why are you not watching Tv with your brothers? "

Baba I don't like to watch horror movies because when I watch them the whole night I can't able to sleep.

Said Sam.

Oh, that's the matter of problem; will talk to them.

After that, he go there and said " Sons can you watch something else? "

Why Baba? Asked Rohan

Because Sam doesn't like to watch these movies

But baba we like this thing only said all

After that, he thought for a while and he said " Do you want to listen to a real perplexed and apprehension story? "

Yes baba every one said in a clangorous way

And Sam also agreed to that.

So, said grandfather today's story which I am going to tell you was a real incident and this story was told by my grandfather.

Oh, It means our grand grandfather said sam

Everyone laughed and said Yes sam

4

Everyone laughed and said Yes sam

CHAPTER TWO

THE ECCENTRIC KILLER

This is the Story of Canada, The date was 1 Jan 1928 in Ottawa the Capital of Canada. That was a Murky night, A Man whose name was Paul, was transiting the road and suddenly he saw that a woman was lying on the road for a while he thought that "why the woman is lying on the road?" Then he goes closer after seeing the woman he was perplexed because there was a slash on the neck and at the time only he understood that it was a homicide! He was trembling because of anxiety, he screamed and said "A woman has been killed by someone!" but that was a late night around 3, everyone was sleeping at their homes. He was very frightened and was not feeling safe, He ran hastily and hastily as much as he can! , Then he came to this home whose no. 1729 when he reached home, he don't waste a second and called the Cops and told everything about the incident but the cops were not believing because till now there was not a single slaying case in the city but Paul was speaking again and again that he saw this from this eyes.

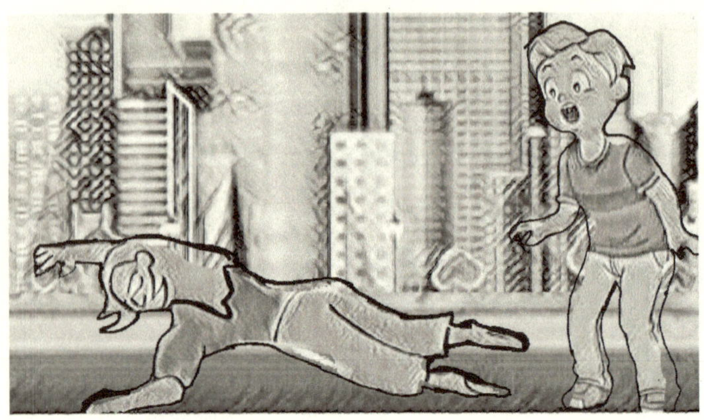

Then cop 81 said, " Well, I don't think that the woman got murdered she can faint but if you are saying a lot then I'm calling at."

After almost 30 min a man named James(The officer) and 2 more cops break up at the place, their eyes were teared up when they saw the woman their eyes went on a cut was on her neck and blood was flowing from that, they straight away call the doctor and when he checked her,

He said " I am Sulked to say that she is dead and her death was not because of that cut but something else which I also can't able to find.

Well, Then how we can let know how she died? Asked James

Sir, I think you should talk to her family said the doctor

After that, they announced about the woman, so that they can find her family. After a day they found her family and they got some information that her name was Komonika and she was coming from her office. But that was not enough information and then they can't find anything else and after that everyone thinks that this can be an accident. After 2 days in the afternoon near the cop station, a cop finds a dead body of a woman. This time everyone was concerned that this was the 2nd death case in this weak. But as usual, they can't find the reason for the death and they also can't able to find the slayer but the similar thing was that on her neck there was the same cut and her name was Komonika.

Like this, within a month there were 8 assassinate of women and the same cut was on everyone's neck and everyone's name was Komonika. Now the people of the city were in terror and people were not coming out of the house, especially the women.

Soon a throng group of people were protesting against the government and cops. After some time the government was coming under pressure.

They ordered James to find that slayer as soon as they can.

James - Guys, Can anyone tell me how we can arrest that perplexing slayer.

Sir, Said cop 164 " We need a person who is smarter than that killer "

Oh, That's a nice idea; But where we can find that man? Asked James

Sir, Said cop 112 " We can take the help of Sir Willam Hawk "

Yea, Now in this bad time he can only help us.

CHAPTER THREE

THE ENTRY OF THE HERO

After that James, Cop 93 and Cop 1 go to the home of Sir Willam Hawk.

Ding Dong (Bell Sound)

The gate opens, there was standing a longwise man with a long bear, his eyes colour was light brownish and that was Sir Willam Hawk.

Oh, James why do you bother to come here? asked Willam

Sir as you know there is an enigmatic slayer who has killed 8 women. said, James

Yea, I also have listened to that news. Said Willam

So, Sir, we need your assistance to catch that slayer because you are a brainiac. So can you help us? said James

He smiled and said " As you can see now I am very old and my brain can't help you in catching that slayer. So I'm regretful...

James interrupted and said, " It means you can't help us?"

Willam bobbed his head in a way to say "Yes"

At the time all the 3 cops were miserable and were almost out of William's home suddenly he stopped all the cops and said " I can't help you but my child Light Hawk help you.

At that time a silver lining again comes into James's heart and was feeling like a million pound

He said " We-Where is he?

At home only said Willam

After that Sir, Willam calls Light Hawk and after a while, Light Hawk breaks up there, He was a young thin long man with black hair and his eyes were blueish

Light Hawk said " What happened, dad?

Son, Officer James needs your help.

Which type of help? asked Light Hawk

As you know from that last some days there is a slayer who is killing women. So James needs that you helped him to glimpse that killer. Said Willam

Oh ok, So I'm ready for that.

After that James and Light Hawk does a handshake.

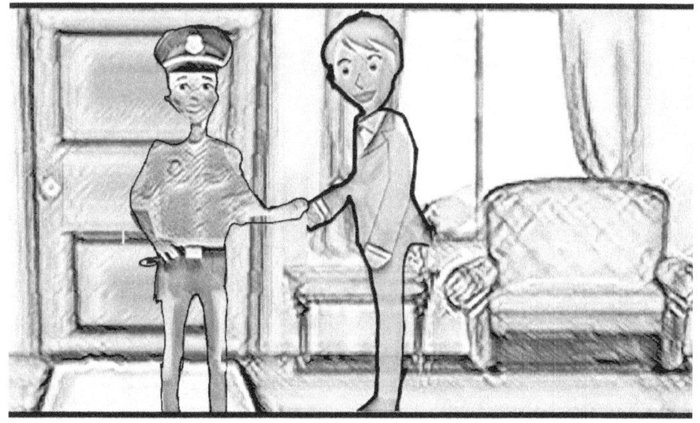

CHAPTER FOUR

Can Light Hawk catch the Slayer?

After that Light Hawk and James go to the cop station and Light Hawk asked

"Officer, can you tell me some details about that slayer?"

Ah... Sir, we don't know anything about that slayer but we know where he killed the women and at what time he killed them.

Oh, that information is enough for me to find that slayer. said Light Hawk assuredly.

Really! James asked in an obligated way

Yes, Can you tell me where he kills them and at what time?

Firstly he killed in the city of Ottawa and then again in the city and after that near a cop station and... again near the city and 5th was also near the city and 6th kill was near a cop station and so on.

Oh okay, and at what time?

Every time we find a body in night or afternoon near 2 to 4 PM.

Oh... ok so give me 2 to 3 hours and I will tell you what to do next.

Ok, Sir.

After almost 1 and half an hour Light hawk call came.

Ring Ring... Ring Ring

Cop 33 do not tarry just pick up the call said James

Yes Sir I'm just picking it.

Light Hawk - Hello Cop 33 can you give the telephone to Officer James

Cop 33 - Yes sir I'm just giving them the call

After that Light Hawk told James that tomorrow slayer will kill a woman near a cop station around 1 to 2 PM.

Oh, so what should we do now?

We have to make 7 small groups of cops as there is 7 cop station in Ottawa city, all the groups will camouflage near the bushes and when he will going kills women we will catch him.

Wow, sir that's a nice idea.

After that they made 7 teams and all cops hide near bushes as their positions.

At 1 PM

Cop 1 - Cop 3 the killer is going to come

Cop 3 - Yea, and be ready with your cannons

Cop 1- Yea Yea I know

At 2 PM

Cop 1- He didn't come till yet.

Cop 2 - Yep, I think in 20 to 30 minutes he will come here

At 3 PM

Cop 1 - Now I am choleric

James - Cop 1 have some forbearance.

Everyone was at their and everyone was talking with their walkie Torquay and after 20 minutes a woman was passing and that killer suddenly appears at the place and all the cops come out from there the place and Light hawk said - Take out your cannons and you killer now you are under arrest

His face was covered with a mask and he wore everything black.

The Killer - Ho-How! Do you catch me?

Light Hawk smiled and said - You are not one of the most intelligent men in the world.

Not that Exactly.

And after that, he throws a capsule and everywhere was smoke and he laughed and said Hahaha Jack can't be arrested.

After that, he started running hastily and hastily.

Light Hawk cried said "Chase Him"

They all get in their cars and start chasing Jack.

After a while, he goes to a footpath and there were some bushes he conceal in that. After that, they all stops their vehicles and came out from that.

Everyone was hushed, After a few seconds, Light Hawk broke the silence and said " Cop 1 and 2 go towards the playground which is after some meters. And else all come with me in the bushes. As they entered in the bushes they came to that playground Light Hawk smiled and said " Ha Ha Ha, I was knowing that he will come into the park and then he will try to escape from here"

And then cop 1 and 2 come into the park with Jack they said " Sir! We caught this slayer.

Nice cop 1 and 2.

After that, they take Jack to the cop station. After some time jack was taken into a room in which there was sitting Light Hawk. He smiled and said, welcome slayer.

HOW DID YOU CATCH ME! He said in an irate way

It's a piece of cake " I was thinking you are a sly man but you are a fool!", I understand your pattern of killing people" First 2 kills were in the city and then near a cop station and this pattern you followed"

Jack saw Light Hawk in a perplexed way and he asked And what about the accurate timing?

Well, It was also a piece of cake, " First kill was in the night around 3 AM and the next was near 3 PM and this pattern you followed" Light Hawk said in a tranquil way.

Oh, You are sharp-witted but not smarter than me, I will escape very easily from here. Said, Jack

Now I have answered your questions, Tell me the answer to 3 Questions

And what if I don't give you the answer.

I will give you a punishment.

My first question is Why did you kill them?

Second, divulge your name

The third is How did you kill them?

Well, I already said to you that I am not going to disclose
my things
Oh then that's fine now you will get penalised.
You can't
Why?
YOU CAN'T!
WHY!
Because I know sorcery.
Really! I don't believe and I know you are lying.
Okay as you wish.

CHAPTER FIVE

THE END OF JACK?

Cop 1! said, Light Hawk

Yes Sir said Cop 1

Take Him to the dungeon and whipped him with a stick till he doesn't tell the answer to my question.

Ok, Sir as you wish.

After that Cop 1 flung jack into the prison and started beating him with the stick.

Sto-Stop cop 1 or I will do back magic and pester your mind!

But cop 1 disregard his warning and started whipping him.

Ah... Ouch... Ahhhhh......

Tell the answers to the questions! said

NO NEVER!

Oh then tolrate the punisment.

Cop1 beat Jack so many times but he didn't tell the answers and now cop 1 was fatigued. He said to Cop 2 " I am going to drink water till then endeavour to ask answer from him.

Ok, will try it.

When he came there after drinking water he saw that Jack was laughing and Cop 2 was wailing.

Wha-what... Happen to you cop 2?

Jack-Jack has done black magic on me.

What! It's impossible.

I am not feeling well.

At the time Cop 1 got Dimply. He doesn't waste a second and ran towards James' room.

Why are you breathing too high?

Officer jack has done Blackmagic on Cop 2

Wha-What!

Yes, I saw this thing with my own eyes.

Oh, So-So what should we do now?

I think we should put him in the gas chamber.

Oh, That's a nice idea.

After that, they put Jack in the chamber where people feel stifled and it's arduous to take oxygen because it is amid harmful gases.

Soon Jack started sounding Ah. Ah. Ah. and then suddenly he falls. For a while no one said anything then cop 2 broke up the silence and said I think we should take out Jack.

Jack fell into the gas chamber

Yea I also think so.

Then they take out jack but he was not taking breathing and when the doctor checked Jack he said " He is no more in the world"

After this news spread like a wildfire in the whole city and everyone was jovial but the cops weren't because they can't able to find the answers to the question that Light Hawk wants to know.

James asked with a scowl way " WHO GIVE THIS IDEA TO PUT JACK IN CHAMBER?

It's Cop 1

Sir let bygones be bygones said Cop 1

Ok, it's fine but what Light Hawk Sir will think?

Only Light Hawk Sir can tell the answer to this question. Said Cop 22

Everyone laughed at cop 22 answer.

After that James Call to Light Hawk
Tring Tring... Tring Tring
Hello What happens, James?
Sir, Jack is dead
What! But How?
Then James told all the things to Light Hawk
Okay, Don't need to worry It's ok, the main thing is that
he is dead means city people are secure
And after that Cops put Jack in the grave.

CHAPTER SIX

JACK GOT HANGED

That was a sweltering day and a man was walking in a sauntered way near Jacks' coffin. And there he saw that a man was coming out of the Coffin!. He screamed and ran hastily from there. After that, he told this thing to the cops.

What!, It's next to impossible! said, James

But, Officer I just saw this thing with my own eyes.

After that Officer with some cops goes towards that coffin. And as saw the coffin they all were stunned. This news was so much startling that it freeze one's blood! All were now very scared and a lot of people started believing that Jack knows black magic.

After that...

Let me call Light Hawk said James, I don't think so he is out of Ottawa and James' guess was correct Light Hawk is in the city! then James call Hawk and told everything to him.

Light Hawk - Okay, That's an engaging case and did you find anything else?

Yes Sir, Inside the coffin there was a paper on which there was written that " Jack never Die!"

Oh Ok, Give me some time I will tell you what to do. Said, Light Hawk

After that Light Hawk goes towards jack's coffin to find some clues and at the time Jack again stated homicides but this time not only women but men were also dying and at a fast rate.

After a day Hawk call James and said " James! We don't have enough time!"

Sir for what?

Jack is going to do a bomb explosion in Ottawa SuperMall around 4:30 PM.

Then James move his head towards the clock and the time was 4:20 PM, It means only 10 minutes are left! James said

YES, THAT'S WHY I'M SAYING WE DON'T HAVE ENOUGH TIME!

Ok, So I am coming with Cops 1 and 2 to the mall

No, Don't need to bring them and don't tell anyone about this thing and come with cop 33 and 44

Ok sir

After that, they reached the place and when Light Hawk checked the time and he saw only 3 minutes were left.

He said - James, Cop 33 and 44 go in different directions and find the bomb and also I know jack is hiding near about.

After that, they all started their mission and a few seconds later Light Hawk found a man who was wearing everything black was hiding near a sofa, he moves his head, he saw that there is a bomb which was a few inches far away from that man. He ran towards the bomb hastily and there were 2 buttons one was green and one red, he was shaking and not understanding what to do and at the time that Black cloaths man said to press the red one but Hawk pressed the green button and the bomb stopped and if Light Hawk was 3 seconds late then it would be blasted.

At the time when Light Hawk stopped the bomb, Jack stand up and started running from there.

COPS CATCH HIM!

And then cops stopped his way and arrested Jack.

James- Light Hawk Sir how did you solve all this enigma?

Light Hawk smiled and said " Actually today when I was coming to the cop station I saw cop1 and 2, they were whispering and I listen that they were saying " Today near 4:30 PM Jack Sir will do a bomb blast in the SuperMarket of Ottawa and I also let to know this egregious man don't know how to do black magic, He gave some money to Cop 1 and 2 do all this drama.

After answering the throng people started clapping for Light Hawk and said LONG LIVE LIGHT HAWK! LONG LIVE LIGHT HAWK!...

After that Officer asked, "Sir may I ask you one more question?"

Yes, why not?

My question is " After the death of Jack how he was still alive?"

As I already told you that Cops 1 and 2 were in Jack's team they gave him a dose from which his nerves stops working for 12 hours and because of that doctor think he is dead.

Wow, Sir, You are an Intellectual man!

And after that Cops 1 and 2 got arrested for 5 years while Jack got the punishment that he will be going to be hanged.

Jack, what's your last wish? Asked Light Hawk

Sir, Why you are asking for a wish? He is a slayer! said, James

James, We should follow the rules, Whether he is a slayer still he is having a right to get a wish. So what's your wish jack?

Ah. Well, will you accept my wish?

Yes

Oh ok, So my wish is that " I will not be hanged on the rope"

What! We can't complete this wish, Tell another which is possible said, Light Hawk

That's not fair

TELL ANOTHER WISH OR WE WILL HANG YOU! Said James in an Enraged way

So, You will hang me the day after tomorrow

Light Hawk smiled and said " Jack you are smart", We are accepting your wish but I am telling you now you can't do anything!

After 2 days Jack got Hanged on Rope.

And that's how the people of Ottawa again started living gleefully.

CHAPTER SEVEN

THE BLAZING MAN

After that, for a month everyday cops go to check Jack's coffin and every day they found him in the coffin only.

After a year...

In Prashu street of Ottawa, A man was walking in an ambling way and his whole body was burning with fire and this all thing captured on a camera.

After that, the cops and people got scared.

Burning Man

After a Day...

Cop 22 tumble up! till now you didn't wake up said Cop 11

ah! What happens? Cop 22 asked in a drowsy way

The officer has given us a commission.

Suddenly Cop 22 stand up and said " Wha-what's that?

Did you hear about that trending news?

Ah. Are you talking about the new movie which has been launched and is very trending? said Cop 22

Off... Cop 22 you always talk about movies and movies!. I am talking about that burning man news.

Oh, Now I understood.

So, Officer James has said that We both have to go to investigation at Prashu street.

Oh, That's an interesting case. Said cop 22

After that, they both go for an examination at the place but miserably they can't able to find a single clue. When they were coming back they were very grumped.

Cop 11- Sir we are back

Did you perceive anything? James asked in an obligated way

N-No Sir said cop 22

Why you both are looking too worried don't be dispirited.

After that days passed and passed, and soon people forgot about that man.

On 25 December 1929 was Christmas day and there were thousands of people gathered to celebrate the festival. But suddenly that burning man started coming towards the gathered people.

Soon he started touching the people and the fire started catching the people. They all started shouting and were running hastily here and there!

The Scene was very horrible.

After a minute that man suddenly vanish and after some time ambulance and cops came there and started assisting the people. Then suddenly cop 3 saw a paper laying on the floor.

W-Wa... What's that! said cop 3

There is paper laying on the floor, Leave that and help the injured people said Cop 12

But Cop 3 heart was saying that the paper is not ordinary, He picked the paper and there was written something and after reading that cop 3 eyes were perplexed, He was too shocked that he was just seeing cop 12

Cop 3 why you are looking in a perplexed way at me?

JACK IS STILL ALIVE. He said in a scary way

What! What are you saying!

See this paper here is write " Jack is still alive hahaha"

And when Cop 12 listened to this thing he was also shocked and can't able to believe it, After that, they all try to track jack's location but as usually they can't able to find his location.

One day when all the cops were relaxing in their police station, suddenly a man came there and that was no one else only that burning man!

Hey, you stop there! said cop 09

But he didn't stop he started touching the walls which were of wood they caught fire and the time one cop took out his pistol and shot him 6 times! but he didn't die. The more cops shot him but not even a scratch came on him.

After that, he started touching the cop too and they all were running here and there but that was too late whole cop station was already burned and there was no way to escape from there. And soon that blazing man vanish.

Soon ambulance came there but till then all the cops were burned up. When this news reached the local people their minds got muddled and many cops left their jobs and many were in dimply.

On that night around 9:00 PM, James was walking here and there in the cop station.

Well, Sir, I want to ask you that for the last 2 hours I'm watching you that you are worried about something, What's that? please share with me. Asked Cop 09

You know why I'm worried not even me the whole city is worried.

Yes sir I know.

Do you have any idea? asked James

Sir only Light Hawk Sir can help us now.

Oh, How fool I am, I don't even think about Light Hawk Sir. He will surely catch that man.

CHAPTER EIGHT

LIGHT HAWK AGAIN IN THE CITY

Ring Ring. Ring Ring...

Light Hawk - Hello; It's Light Hawk, whose is there?

James - Hello Sir, It's me James

Hawk - Oh, Hello James is everything fine there?

James - No Sir, There is a Buring Man who is very perilous.

Hawk - What!, Burning Man?

Yes Sir, After that James told all the things to Light Hawk

Well, I will come but after 2 days because I am solving a case in India

Oh Ok Sir, Till then will try to catch him

After 2 days at 5:45 AM, Light Hawk landed at the airport of Ottawa City.

After that, he go to the cop station and asked James

Can you tell me Something about Blazing Man?

Ah... Sir, he wore everything black and his head was also covered by something which I can't able to see because of fire.

Okay, And did you check Jacks Coffin?

No Sir

What! You don't even check Jacks Coffin after seeing that paper!

N-N-No Sir

It means Jack again Escaped from there. Give me a Day after that I will tell you what to do.

After a Day...

Light Hawk reached the cop station and said to James

We have to hurry up.

What Happened Sir?

We need an Iron Cage which will trap Jack and we have to do it as soon as it can be possible because tomorrow Jack will go to burn the Super Market.

Ok Sir, So I am buying the Iron Cage

After that James buy one of the strongest cages in the city and told this thing to Hawk.

So, Sir what do we have to do now?

We have to place this Iron cage on a tree in such a way that he doesn't think it's a trap.

The Next Day, They all were hiding in the bushed and Light Hawk was behind the tree.

After some time Blazing Man passes from there and when he comes in front of the tree and at the time only Light Hawk cut the rope and that blazing man got trapped in the cage.

Oh, Here you are said, Light Hawk

Now burn cop station said Cop 07 in an angry way

At the time James was feeling very happy and then he thanked Light Hawk and asked how did you able to know that he will come here, Sir?

Haha, It's a piece of cake, When I visited Jacks' coffin, I found someone lying in it and I think it was Jack but it was not looking like Jack and guess what, It was a dummy and when I removed it there was a tunnel, I go deeper in it and I reached in a house there was bord and on that there was written Future Plans and from that, I let to know this all.

Wow, Sir, that's splendid!

So it's you Jack? asked Cop 7

But there was no reply. Then Light Hawk bring 3 buckets of Water and flung them on Blazing Man and after some time the fire got extinguished. Then they arrested Him and take him to the cop station. But when they removed the mask they let to know that it was not Jack! but someone else.

Who-Who are you? asked Hawk

I will never tell you

Oh, then we have to torment you! Get a bucket of water and electricity.

Then they give electricity to him

Burning   Man   "

AH.AH.AH.AHHHHHHHHHHHHHHHHHHHHHHH"   ,

ok ah. ok I will tell

Then they stopped the electricity.

Tell me who are you? James asked

I-I am Jack 2

What Jack 2?

Yes, I work for Jack and after completing my task he gave me money.

How many people Do work for Jack? asked Hawk

I don't know about that but I think more than 1000 people.

What! And how is Jack still alive?

Suddenly Cop 6 said Don't tell Light Hawk about me

What! You to from Jack team! asked James

Yes, He is and Cop 6 and Cop 5 helped Jack to escape. said Jack 2

But we hanged him on rope still he was safe how?

He got helped by Both of them and they make the rope a bit loose so he was safe like that. said Jack 2

Arrest Both the Cop! James ordered to cop 4

And tell why you were not dying? Asked Hawk

I was not dying because...

Suddenly bullets sound came from somewhere. After a while

W-What was that! Jack. Jack2!

Jack 2 was dead because of the bullets, 2 bullets were shot at Jack's head

At the time only Hawk's eyes go towards the window from where the bullets were shot and at that time only he saw a man in the black jacket running from there.

Hawk stood up and ran towards at door of the cop station but till then that man has vanished. He saw 2 cops standing at the door, he said " Why are you standing silently here? , A man came and shoot towards the cop station and you both were just watching him!

Cop 55 - N-No Sir, we were just going to catch Jack Sir.

What! Jack Sir?, How do you know that he was Jack? asked Hawk

No reply comes from Cop 55 side.

Then Cop 56 broke up the silence and said "Sir please forgive us, now we will not work for Jack, Please sir. Please"

It means you both are also in Jack's team! said, James

Yes Sir

Take them in custody! said, Hawk

OK Sir

After that.

Why do you work for Jack! Asked James

A... Because we want that this city should be ruled by Convicts. Said Cop 55

What! never it can't be ruled by Serial killers till then me and Light Hawk sir is there!

Wait, James, have some patients. said, Hawk. Tell, How many more Cops are corrupted like you?

Um. Well, I don't know exactly how many corrupted cops are there but according to estimation, more than 300 cops are corrupted. Said Cop 56

O My God 300! , It means only 10% of Cops are not corrupted said James in a stunning way

That's a very miserable thing said Hawk in a lamentable way

Where is Jack's headquarters? asked Hawk

We don't know the exact place but it's underground replied Cop 55

Why you don't know?

Because when we have to meet Jack they first put the blindfold on our eyes and then we meet him.

Okay, So anything else you know about Jack?

NO

After that, they both got 10 years of prison punishment

CHAPTER NINE

A PLANE OF KILLING HAWK

After that, One day Light Hawk was talking with James and at that time he saw a man coming to their cop station and he was breathlessness?

What happens?

Light. Light Hawk Sir you are in peril!

Wh-What! How...How I am in trouble?

Jack is going to kill you after 2 days when you will give a speech at The Central Mall of Ottawa.

What's your name? and How did you know that so?

My name is Obheek and I work for Jack

Cop 4 arrest him right now! said, James

Wait cop 4, James why are you punishing him?

Sir, he works for Jack

But he is saving me from Jack's plan, and After some seconds Light Hawk asked " What are you saving me? "

Because if you will die then who will save Ottawa from Jack.

Well, Then why did you join Jack's army?

Because I was not having money early at the time one man came and said to me " Will you Join Jack's army" and that's why I joined his company

Okay, So what is the plan for killing me?

When Jack came into headquarters he said to us " Day after tomorrow Light Hawk will come at Super Market of Ottawa for giving the speech and I want that we will kill him there so that Ottawa will be ours, so my plan one is that we have found a duplicate of James who looks same as James, as he will be behind of Light Hawk we will give me one knife from which he will kill him and if you all talk about real James, we will kidnap him!...

James interrupted and said "What! Jack will Kidnap me, I will arrest him and I will hang him on the rope!"

Wait James let me listen to what happens next

So shall I continue Sir? asked Obheek

Yes Yes

After that, he said " If somehow he got safe for that I have plan B in which I have placed some underground TNT in his way and when he will put his legs on the ground where TNT has been placed that TNT will blast up and then he will die. But then also he got secure from that I have my last plan and this plan I will tell only to whom I trusted". After that Jack and some people go into a secret room. So sir in my opinion you should not go for a speech.

Yes Sir he is right said, James

Light Hawk grinned and said " I am contented and very thankful for telling me all these things but I will go there and before going there with the help of Dogs we will let to know where Jack places more bombs and his 3rd plane will not be too dangerous because Jack doesn't have that much brain

But Sir...

Don't worry James, I will come safely. And what you have to do is to announce that you are on 1-day leave and you are not sure that you can join the day after tomorrow's speech, if you come on time to Ottawa so you will join and if you can't then you will not join. And then without kidnapping you, they all will come and I will catch Jack there. And Obheek doesn't leave Jack's company you can help us in future.

After 2 days...

Before going to Super Market Hawk met James and asked " How was the trip? "

Ah. That was nice

When he listened to James's words he grinned because his voice was different and it means that was phoney James.

After that, before entering the mall suddenly phoney James move his knife toward Light Hawk and what's that! Light Hawk doesn't even notice and James hit that knife in Hawk's back but he don't even get a scratch, the time Light Hawk laughed and said " Haha I was knowing that you are phoney James now you are under arrest.

H-How have you got safe?

I was wearing armour.

Oh Shit!

And then He got under arrest, after some seconds one cop broke up the silence and said " What was that sir? A fake James I don't think so you should give a speech here you are not safe.

Don't worry, I know everything that will happen next.

oh. So shall we go now?

Yes, but not from here because in front of me there are some TNT placed and if I step there then I will die.

Then they all go from another site and then some cop dig inside and yes there were some TNT

One.two.three.four.five... Oh My God 15 TNTs! said Cop93 in a shooking way

Let's remove these TNT from here.

Then Light Hawk came on stage and a lot of people were there, they were chearing Hawk and then he started his speech and what's that! the gun sound came and Light Hawk feels like he has just got shooted by a bullet and

everyone was running here and there.

CHAPTER TEN

Is Light Hawk Still Alive?

Ahh...W-Who are you? and W-We-Where I am? asked Hawk

Oh. Sir you...you regain consciousness said Doctor is a contented way

Wh-What! How-How I am here?

Ah. Sir that's a long story.

So-So tell me

Yes Sir, So on the day when you come to the supermarket in Ottawa for giving the speech, So you were saved from the first 2 traps of Jack but when you started your speech suddenly some shot bullets and 2 of them hit your head and you started running here and there and at the time one bullet hit your leg and then you faint we take you here, at the time everyone was thinking that now you are dead but you are the luckiest one

How?

Because in this situation only 1 got to save in thousand of people.

Oh, But from where the bullet got shot?

When you were standing there was a small hole at roof from which bullet got shoot

Okay, It means that this was the plane C of Jack.

Yes, So should I tell this incredible news to everyone that you are still alive?

NO

Why Sir

Because till now I am not fully recovered.

But for the last 3 months, criminals cases are increased in the city!, So if you don't tell now you are well then the criminal cases will increase as usual

But if you told that I am now well then they will try to kill me again, so tell the news that I am dead so that Jack will do all the crimes without any alertness and it will be easy to catch him

And soo this news preached to whole city and criminals cases also increased and when this news reaches to James he was very lamentable and lost all hopes. After a week Light Hawk was all right, he thanked the Doctor and left the hospital. After that, he reached the Cop station where

James was sitting sadly as Light Hawk entered the Cop station, One Cop said " Hey...Wh-What! it's the ghost of Light hawk sir. " and as soon as James has seen Light Hawk he screamed and said " ghost!"

No James, I am not ghost

Ho-How can I believe; Light Hawk sir has died last week

That was a piece of fake news

What! Fake news

Yes, I said to tell this fake news so that Jack will not going to try to kill me as I was not well at the time

O my God, It means now you are well and can catch the slayer, earlier I was thinking you are a ghost

So as you know nowadays a lot of criminals cases are coming in the city and now Jack is not taking that many precautions so we can catch him easily. said, Hawk

Yea, But how are we will going to know where he will go to do the crime?

We can take the help of Obheek

Who's Obheek?

Obheek? You don't even remember him

Uhh... No

He told me all about Jack's plan of killing me!

Oh. Yea now I remembered

So, We will ask him now where Jack is going to do the crime.

But now not only Jack but more criminals are in the city and they are trying to make their separate country said, James

Yes, Don't worry we will first catch Jack and then else criminals.

Ok sir, But.

Again But!

Si-Sir I have the last question where we are going to find Obheek?

I already have his address, and we will go in normal clothes.

But why?

Ah. Well because there can be more people who work in Jack's company because if you wear a cop dress then they will know you and by knowing you they will know me too and then Jack will be alerted.

After that Light Hawk and James go into Obheek's home in normal clothes as they reached his home and knock on Obheek's Home the gate didn't open

Sir, Why his gate is not opening?

Um. I think he is not at his home

So, Should we wait here?

We have to, as we don't have any other option.

Then They sat near the house and wait for him, After some time a wise man came there who was looking very old and having a long beer.

He asked them " Of whom you are waiting of? "

Uh...Uh, James whisper

Suddenly Light Hawk interrupted and said " We are waiting for someone"

Oh, The owner of this house?

Um. Yea said, Hawk

Okay, It means Obheek

Do you know him? James asked

Yes, I live here only and when I from a long time I am watching you and was thinking that "of whom you are waiting for?"

Oh, So can you tell us when he will come? asked Hawk

Around 10 PM.

Ok thanks

After that when that Man goes from there, James said to hawk " It's 4:45 and we have to wait for more than 5 hours"

Yes, But if we have to catch Jack so we have to wait for Obheek.

After that around 10 PM, a man came near Obheek's house and when he saw Hawk and James he said " Who are you ?"

I-I am James and this is Light Hawk Sir James said in a drowsy way

Wha-What! Light Hawk! He was dead a week ago

No, That was fake news Obheek said, Light Hawk

After listening to this Obheek legs started trembling and sweat started coming out of his head. That's Impossible!

No, my friend, That was a piece of fake news and see my voice isn't the same as Light Hawk?

Um. Yes your voice, body language and Face are the same as Hawk

Okay that's nice

After that Obheek welcomed them in his miniature home

After that, they all came into Obheek's house and Hawk said " Obheek, I want to know that now where Jack will do crime and at what time?

Ah. I think tomorrow at 12 PM

Where?

In Prashu street of Ottawa, I am not sure about the time and how he will do a crime there.

Okay, That's enough information and thanks for telling

Your welcome Sir

After that Hawk and James leave Obheek's House.

While coming back to the Cop station James asked Hawk " Sir which type of crime Jack can do.

Um... He will do a normal crime as he knows that I am dead, so it will be easier to catch him.

O so tomorrow Jack's game will end and how many cops we should take with us? Asked James

Not much. Because most of them are corrupted.

Ok Sir, So will reach early there as we don't know when Jack will come there

All right, We will reach there at 5 AM in the morning said, Hawk

Can't we go at 6?

James! Time and Tide wait for none so will go at 5 only

The next day...

Cold wind was blowing and everyone was ready with their guns and stick.

So, Let's go to Prashu Street said, Light Hawk

As they reached there they saw a throng of people was there with guns by seeing them Cops understood that it was Jack's team and after half a minute some more people came there and they were wearing different clothes it means that was a different team and soon they all started shooting here and there and fire some houses. People ran here and there hastily! Then Light Hawk said "Attack on them!"

Bu-But ho-how we can fight them, they are large in quantity said a Cop

If you have fear of fighting them then why did you choose this job! If you want you can come with me and if don't then get lost! Attack my army! Light Hawk screamed and then all the cops started shooting at criminals and soon they all also started shooting at cops, that was a bloody conflict from everywhere gun sound was coming; By the time a bullet hits James' hand and a lot of blood was flowing from there" Ah...Ah"

Wh-What happen James? Light Hawk asked, A-a-a bullet hit your hand! Let me take you to the doctor

N-n-no need s-sir I am fine, I-i will fight till my last breath.

Light Hawk's eyes felt with tears and at the time he was very angry. He started shooting at a rapid rate and soon a lot of people started running from there and that's how they won that fight but at a high cost they lost their 10 cops and 5 were injured! while 37 criminals were dead. But Hawk was not happy because he can't catch or kill Jack and also lost 10 cops.

CHAPTER ELEVEN

THE DEATH OF WILLAM HAWK

After that, all 5 cops were admitted to Hospital, 4 of them were not that injured but James was very injured and he need blood as a lot of blood was already flowing out from his body

Hey, We need some blood, James what's your blood group? asked Doctor

But no reply came from James

Oh no, He is faint, Now what we can do? Did anyone else know his blood group?

The doctor gives him the blood of O-, Said Hawk

Are you sure? asked Doctor

Doctor, I don't exactly know his blood group but one day He told me his blood was negative.

But there are a lot of negative blood groups, so how you can say it's 0-

Well, As you know O negative blood is fine for everyone.

Oh, Why I don't think about that, Sir you are accurate, Let me give him O negative blood.

After an hour James's eyes opened and he said " Where I am? " and then Hawk told him everything to James.

Oh, So did we win that war? asked James

Yes but no

What are you trying to say, Sir?

We win but at a high cost we lost our 10 cops

Oh, Sir but don't be disappoint

Yea I know, but we can win that war more easily if we go with better planning and we would not lose our 10 cops.

When the doctor saw James he said " Oh finally you are fine but my advice is to stay in hospital for a month.

Wa-what I can't stay in hospital for a month, I have to help Light Hawk Sir in catching Jack.

James's health is more important than anything else said, Hawk.

Suddenly a call came " ring...ring ring"

When Light Hawk pick up the call, his eyes were full of tears and was angry Inside in a while his face became red.

What happens, Sir? James asked

M-m-my dad is de-dead

Wh-What! How?

No reply came from the Light hawk's side, He ran from there, A day passed but no sign of Light Hawk was there nor he was at home.

After 2 days a piece of breaking news came on the news channel of Ottawa that Jack's headquarters got divulged and thousands of people got caught, who worked for Jack and this was all done by Light Hawk

After listening to this news James said to the doctor "What! Light Hawk Sir finds Jack's headquarters, It's Impossible"

Who said it's Impossible? said, Light Hawk

Wh-What! Sir when you came

Just Now

Sir, please tell me everything that what's going on. Now I am puzzled

Okay, So listen, The day before yesterday when a call came for me, A cop told me that my dad is no more in the world, me at the time not able to believe this thing and then I got to my home and there was a throng of people and when I entered there in the house on the front door, my-my dad was lying and...

What Happened, Sir, Why did you stop?

I-i can't tell what happens next.

And then Hawk's eyes fill with tears and hawk said " And I saw that my father's ey-eyes were not the-there...

Wh-What! How

And then Hawk's face became angry and he said " There was a paper on a table near my dad and in that, there was written " I have taken you Dad's eyes Hawk and will think what to do with it, I can't able to kill you but it's not arduous to kill your dad. It's me, Jack"

And after that, I was too angry and all I wanted was to kill Jack at the time I let know some of my friends who are detectives are in another city near Ottawa and they all were just chilling so I call at their place and told them everything and now I and 17 other detectives were ready to kill Jack.

James Intruped and said " Why you don't take the help of cops? "

For this question, I can give you an answer to one word " Corruption! "

Okay

So then I went to Obheek and there I asked him how he reaches Jack's headquarters and he told me that every morning at 5 AM a man came there and put a blindfold on him and then he sat on a jeep and he is taken to Jack's headquarters...

Wait, James interrupted, We can do this same thing early to catch Jack.

Yea, But at the time I didn't think about this thing...

So I said to him that "next day when you will get to Jack's headquarter we will be behind your Jeep". So next day in the morning they took Obheek in the Jeep and there were 3 more people who were wearing blindfolds and a man was driving the car and one more man was there with a pistol. So after an hour, the jeep stopped and at the time we were in a village near Ottawa city, There were a lot of small huts and they all went to one of them, as they entered there, they remove 3 square boxes which were lying on the floor and then there was something from which they go inside but we can't able to see that, after a while, we went there and there were leaders, soon we went down and we were ready without guns too.

As we went into it there was a big lab and some people were experimenting suddenly someone saw us and he said " Who are you? "

We were not having any answer for that all were looking here and there and then he understood that we were not a part of Jack's team, he screamed and said " Some people have come here and will kill us! "

At the time we didn't understand what to do now? I take out my gun and said " If you move from your place you will be shot by us" then a siren started shouting and all started running here and there, I said to 3 of my friends to block the entrance of the lab and then we all ran from there and started finding Jack but that was too late, He ran from there in front of us and a cloud of smoke started flowing and some members of Jack headquarter started feeling on the floor and It was looking like harmful gas and I was correct, I saw here and there and I found some face covered mask I throw some of them towards my friends and one of it I wore and thankfully we got save and we arrested thousands of people and some people ran from there and that's how we find Jack's headquarter and arrested thousands of people.

Wow, Sir, you are a genius.

And at the time a man came there and broke up the silence and said " And we found some chemicals and which Jack was going to use on to kill cops and government people.

Who is he? asked James

He is my friend "Aarush" and he helped me yesterday

Oh, Hello Sir

Hello James

Can you give your introduction Sir?

I am Aarush. Me and Light Hawk are one of the famous Indian Detectivee.

Oh. that's nice, So can you both tell me anything else you find there?

Oh, Yea. We found a bomb with was having a lot of gunpowder and I am sure it was going to use for any big bomb blast. said, Hawk

So, Where it is right now? asked James

It's in the lab of Ottawa said Aarush

And we found a very good thing there said, Hawk

What's that?

Some Bulletproof vests which will protect us and we have sent to a secret lab where we will let to know how to make them.

Light Hawk, said Aarush " Till now I don't understand that from where he got so much money for make lab as he is not a robber and from where he able to know that how to make these things as no one till now knows that"

Yea Aarush, this is a mystery yet and like this, we can't able to find that how Jack 2 was alive when he was burning.

CHAPTER TWELVE

JACK'S RIGHT HAND GOT ARRESTED

After some days James got discharged from the hospital, A lot of local people came there and were very contented and when James came out of the hospital people clapped for him. James was feeling very proud and he thanked all the people. After that Light Hawk and James go to the cop station

After a long time, watching my cop station said James

As they entered the cop station there was standing Obheek

Obheek? Why are you here? asked James, Oh I know you are here for me

N-no Sir, Me and some cops arrested Robert

Who's that? asked Hawk

He is the right hand of Jack

What! Right Hand of Jack but where you find him asked James

When I and some cop were doing investigation we found Robert entering the lab and taking a capsule from there and was almost out of the lab but we caught him.

Well done Obheek, So where he is right now? asked Hawk

He is in prison.

After that, they took Robert into custody and Light Hawk asked Now you can't escape so it's good to tell whatever I am going to ask or we will torment you.

Yea, I know I can't escape but I am loyal to Jack I will don't tell anything

After that Light Hawk go closer to Robert and said something in his ears and no one can able to listen to anything.

Ok, I will tell you said, Robert

At the time everyone was shocked and was thinking that what Hawk had said.

Tell me where is Jack right now

Um. 3 days earlier when I call Jack, he told me that "he is thinking of going to the USA but the problem was if he will be outside then people will know him and he will be arrested and he told me that he will go to Gatineau City which is 6 Km far away from there".

Okay, Is he going with his team?

I don't think so, as it's broken up, And he will not going to trust anyone

So, in my opinion, he should be in Gatineau City only said Obheek

Um. He can be or can't be.

We should send Cops there said, James

No, said Hawk, If we send cops there he will hide in the secret place and we will not able to find him.

So, What should we do? asked Obheek

We will send cops but not in cop dress, they will go in normal dress up.

Ok, sir, said James

I think Jack's end is near said Obheek

Yes, But remember don't be overconfident and by tomorrow send 100 cops there and remember James place some cops at the exit of Gatineau.

Ok sir, As you wish

After that 157 Cops came to Gatineau along with James and Hawk, they both stay in a home with was near the exit of Gatineau City. The next day there were a lot of people who were there to go out from the city and at the time James said "I am going to check all the people there"

No, Don't go there said, Hawk

Why?

Because if Jack will be there then he will see you and he will understand everything and he will escape from there.

If I will don't check then he can escape from there

After that Hawk move his head here and there and after a while, he said " We will watch all people with the nearby window from which we can get a clear view.

Oh, yea that's a nice idea.

After that, they both fixed their eyes on the window and were watching everyone who was going from there. After some time Hawk's eyes go to a man whose face was covered with a mask and when Hawk saw him he was looking different from other people and was looking like Jack.

James this man is looking like Jack, his body language, and posture were looking like Jack.

So, We should catch him.
Yep

CHAPTER THIRTEEN

JACK'S THE END

They both came out from there and ran towards Jack at the same time Jack's eyes goes on them he started running hastily and at the time Light Hawk's heart was saying that they can't catch Jack but he believed in himself was tracking Jack.

Hey, you Jack stop! Stop! or I will shoot a bullet said, James

But no reply came from Jack's side and he was running continuously.

And then James shoots a bullet on Jack's leg and Jack falls " Ahh. Ahh Jack was murmuring "

Oh, Sad If you listen to James' words then you were not feeling like this. Hawk said

Ah... Finally, you catch me... Ah, now what you will do with me?

I Will tell you later, James let's take him to Cop Station and then they hold Jack tightly and sat in the car. Then they went to the hospital and the next day they brought Jack to the cop station and then Light Hawk flung him in custody.

So Jack, Now you can't escape anymore and today's your last day but before that, I want to know the answer to some mystery.

Um. Yea now I know I can't be safe so I can only give you the answer to my mystery from the heart I don't want to give the answers but I don't want that I will die because of torment.

So, tell me who are you? and tell me your actual name.

I warn you earlier only when I will tell my name and who I am you can be faint.

Just tell!

My name is Paul and I was a local man of Ottawa and my house no.1729

And as James listen to this he was perplexed and was stopped at the place where he was standing and looking like he was a statue and was looking at Jack continuously.

Haha... I was knowing it. James will be astonished by listening to this.

B-But what's the shocking thing in this answer?

Ask James said, Jack

Jam-James. James!

And suddenly James' eyes blinked and said Ye-Yes Sir?

Why you were shocked?

Be-Because " He was the only one who call us and told us about Komonika who was dead and we met him at his home too whose address was 1729.

What! that's terrible! said Hawk stunningly, That was unexpected Jack, bu-but why did you start killing women?

Because when I was a local person who does the job in a factory, one day when I was coming home in between there was a madwoman named Komonika was there with some cops and she was crying as her child was dead and as she saw me she said to cop " He-He has killed my son, he. he is that." and at the time I told them that I was not that man but they don't believe me and they arrested me for 2 years and when I was in prison I take an oath that now I will kill her and all the women named Komonika and that's how I became a slayer.

Oh so sad, bu-but you should not take this criminal path and that's like you did Tit for Tat

At the time I have chosen that path but now I can't do anything, time is not in my control.

Um. So " How was Jack 2 still alive after his cloaths were burning? "

Oh, I made an armour which was transparent and if you wear it and you place fire then also armour will save you.

But from where you're able to make this armour and of what it was made?

I use my brain for making this and I will never tell this thing that how I made that and if you are going to kill me then also I will not going to tell you.

You are so weird. Ok, I will not be going to ask for that as you are telling me all answers. So my last question is where did you get a lot of money from which you were able to make an underground lab, and can able to give salaries to scientists, cops and other people and why did you not stop your crimes after killing 8 Komonika named women?

Suddenly Jack started laughing very loudly and creepy and said " After killing them, I started loving to kill people and I got a lot of money from the government and some terrorist groups

What! from the government how! It-It means there were corrupted people in government. asked James

YES!

No way, That's very disappointing said James and Hawk at the same time.

Off, But! now you will be hanged, Jack! said Hawk angerly

And then Jack got Hanged on the rope and that's how a small Jack era got to end. And again whole country people started living happily and Light Hawk (An egghead) became one of the most Intelligent detectives in the world and people of the world always remember him.

Wow-what a thrilling and mysterious story that was said, Sam

See, this is more interesting than a horror film said, grandfather

Grandfather, I didn't understand a thing that "What Light Hawk said to Robert that he told him all the answers" said Pranjal

Oh yea, That's still a mystery

But grandfather then what Light Hawk did

Um. that's a long story will tell you in next winter breaks and suddenly grandfathers eyes goes on the clock that was 11 PM and next day all the 4 kids have to arrive at their home.

And that's how winter breaks end and all the brothers go back to their homes.

Glossary

1. Murky - Gloomy or dark
2. Obligated - Excited
3. Dreaded - Fear
4. Perplexed - Puzzled
5. Apprehension - suspense
6. Trill - loud
7. Enigmatic - Mysterious
8. Transiting - crossing
9. Slash - Cut, typically using a knife
10. Homicide - Murder
11. Trembling - shaking
12. Anxiety - fear
13. Screamed - make a loud, high-pitched sound.
14. slaying - killing
15. Sulked - Sad
16. concerned - worried
17. Assassinate - Murder
18. Terror - extreme fear.
19. Throng - a large group of people
20. Slayer - someone who kills a person or animal in a violent way
21. assistance - help
22. regretful - sorry
23. bobbed - to move quickly up and down
24. miserable - sadly
25. glimpse - catch
26. assuredly - confidently
27. tarry - delay
28. choleric - irritated

29. forbearance - presence
30. Frosty - Cold
31. Divulge - reveal
32. Penalised - punishment
33. dungeon - Prison
34. whipped - beat
35. Flung - throw forcefully
36. endeavour - try
37. wailing- to cry or complain in a loud, high voice, especially because you are sad or in pain
38. Dimply - small depression
39. stifled - suffocated
40. amid - surrounded
41. jovial - happy
42. sweltering - uncomfortable hot
43. Hastily - fast
44. Stunned - shocked
45. engaging - intresting
46. enigma - mystery
47. Intellectual - Intelligent
48. Enraged - Angry
49. gleefully - happily
50. Blazing - Burning
51. ambling - to walk at a slow relaxed speed
52. Tumble up - to wake up
53. drowsy - sleepy
54. commission - task
55. grumped - sad
56. dispirited - disappointed
57. muddled - disturbed
58. perilous - dengerous
59. Convicts - criminals
60. regain - recover

61. lamentable - sad
62. peril - great danger
63. precautions - something that you do now in order to avoid danger or problems in the future
64. miniature - small
65. murmuring - to say something in a low quiet voice